CLASSIC
POEMS
FOR CHILDREN

The Compiler

Nicola Baxter has written or compiled over three hundred titles. She has developed ideas for a wide variety of international publishers and particularly enjoys the marriage of words and pictures.

The Illustrator

Cathie Shuttleworth was trained in calligraphy, heraldry and illumination. Through her work with the Royal College of Arms, she has produced coats of arms for the wedding of HRH Prince Andrew and worked on other royal projects, but her real love is book illustration.

CLASSIC
POEMS
FOR CHILDREN

BEST-LOVED VERSE FROM THE GREAT POETS, INCLUDING LEWIS CARROLL, JOHN KEATS AND WALT WHITMAN

ARMADILLO

This edition is published by Armadillo, an imprint of Anness Publishing Ltd,
Hermes House, 88–89 Blackfriars Road, London SE1 8HA;
tel. 020 7401 2077; fax 020 7633 9499
www.annesspublishing.com

If you like the images in this book and would like to investigate using them for publishing, promotions or advertising,
please visit our website www.practicalpictures.com for more information.

UK distributor: Book Trade Services; tel. 0116 2759086; fax 0116 2759090;
uksales@booktradeservices.com; exportsales@booktradeservices.com
North American distributor: National Book Network; tel. 301 459 3366; fax 301 429 5746; www.nbnbooks.com
Australian distributor: Pan Macmillan Australia; tel. 1300 135 113; fax 1300 135 103; customer.service@macmillan.com.au
New Zealand distributor: David Bateman Ltd; tel. (09) 415 7664; fax (09) 415 8892

Publisher: Joanna Lorenz
Editor: Elizabeth Young
Compiler: Nicola Baxter
Illustrator: Cathie Shuttleworth
Production Controller: Don Campaniello

Previously published in two separate volumes *The Children's Classic Poetry
Collection* and *Classic Poetry for Children*

ETHICAL TRADING POLICY

At Anness Publishing we believe that business should be conducted in an ethical and ecologically sustainable way,
with respect for the environment and a proper regard to the replacement of the natural resources we employ.
As a publisher, we use a lot of wood pulp in high-quality paper for printing, and that wood commonly comes from
spruce trees. We are therefore currently growing more than 750,000 trees in three Scottish forest plantations:
Berrymoss (130 hectares/320 acres), West Touxhill (125 hectares/305 acres) and Deveron Forest
(75 hectares/185 acres). The forests we manage contain more than 3.5 times the number of trees
employed each year in making paper for the books we manufacture.
Because of this ongoing ecological investment programme, you, as our customer, can have the pleasure
and reassurance of knowing that a tree is being cultivated on your behalf to naturally replace
the materials used to make the book you are holding.
Our forestry programme is run in accordance with the UK Woodland Assurance Scheme (UKWAS) and
will be certified by the internationally recognized Forest Stewardship Council (FSC). The FSC is
a non-government organization dedicated to promoting responsible management of the world's forests.
Certification ensures forests are managed in an environmentally sustainable and socially responsible way.
For further information about this scheme, go to www.annesspublishing.com/trees

PUBLISHER'S NOTE

Although the advice and information in this book are believed to be accurate and true at the time of going to press, neither
the authors nor the publisher can accept any legal responsibility or liability for any errors or omissions that may be made.

Contents

Animals and Birds

The Owl and the Pussy-Cat 12
Jabberwocky 14
Hurt No Living Thing 16
How Doth the Little Crocodile 17
Auguries of Innocence 18
The Herring Loves the Merry Moonlight 20
The Maldive Shark 21
My Cat Jeoffry 22
The Owl 24
The Silver Swan 25
The Tyger 26
The Eagle 27

Weather and Seasons

Whether the Weather Be Fine 30
It's Raining, It's Pouring 31
The Rainbow 32
The Wind 33
The North Wind Doth Blow 34
Windy Nights 35
The Human Seasons 36
Winter 37
Spring 38
From Rain in Summer 40
Fall, Leaves, Fall 41
The Year's at the Spring 42

Bright and Beautiful

Pied Beauty 44
My Shadow 45
Daffodils 46
The Echoing Green 48
She Walks in Beauty 50
Shall I Compare Thee to a Summer's Day? 51
Blow, Bugle, Blow 52

Dreams and Wonders

Kubla Khan 54
The Fairies 57
La Belle Dame Sans Mercie 60
I Saw a Peacock 63
A Child's Thought 64

Songs of the Sea

Full Fathom Five 66
What Are Heavy? 67
I Started Early 68
O Captain! My Captain! 70
Break, Break, Break 72
Meeting at Night 73

Tales of Travel

Ozymandias 76
Where Lies the Land? 77
Eldorado 78
Foreign Lands 80
Uphill 81
Travel 82
From a Railway Carriage 84

Childhood

Little Orphant Annie 86
Monday's Child 88
A Child's Grace 89
I Remember, I Remember 90
Swing, Swing 92
Good and Bad Children 93

At the End of the Day

Escape at Bedtime 96
Bed in Summer 97
Is the Moon Tired? 98

Wynken, Blynken, and Nod 99
How Many Miles to Babylon? 101
Star Light, Star Bright 101
Hush Little Baby 102
Sleep, Baby, Sleep! 103

Love and Adventure

Robin Hood 106
A Red, Red, Rose 107
A Birthday 108
Lochinvar 109
A New Courtly Sonnet of the Lady Greensleeves 112
The Night Has a Thousand Eyes 115

Songs and Ballads

Thomas the Rhymer 118
Bonny Barbara Allan 122
The Great Silkie of Sule Skerrie 124
The Yarn of the *Nancy Bell* 126

Boys and Girls

What Am I After All 132
Jemima 133
There Was a Naughty Boy 134
The False Knight and the Wee Boy 136
Children 138
When That I Was and a Little Tiny Boy 140

Magic and Mystery

Waltzing Matilda 144
The Ghost's Song 146
John Barleycorn 147
A Strange Visitor 151
The Oxen 154

Sights and Sounds

Upon Westminster Bridge 156
On First Looking into Chapman's Homer 157
Symphony in Yellow 158
A Thing of Beauty 159
From The Garden 160

Music and Dancing

Song's Eternity 162
The Power of Music 165
Piano 166
I Am of Ireland 167
To Emilia V – 168

Sadness and Happiness

So, We'll Go No More A-Roving 170
Spring and Fall *to a young child* 171
Canadian Boat Song 172
In the Highlands 174
When in Disgrace with Fortune 176
Piping Down the Valleys Wild 177
A Lark's Nest 178
From The Song of Solomon 179
The Swing 180
Requiem 181

About the Poets 184

Glossary 188

Index of Titles and First Lines 190

Introduction

In this collection of classic poems, you will encounter old favourites such as Edward Lear's '*The Owl and The Pussy-Cat*' nestled alongside lesser known poems like '*I Started Early*' by Emily Dickinson. These are works that everyone can enjoy reading aloud; share and discuss the various themes or simply sit and read together. There are poems for reflection, some to make you laugh and others that will make you cry. This inspirational book is designed to introduce readers of all ages to poetry, it is the starting point on a very special journey through time to a whole spectrum of thoughts and feelings, magical lands and far-away places. We very much hope you enjoy it.

ANIMALS
and
BIRDS

The Owl and the Pussy-Cat

The Owl and the Pussy-Cat went to sea
In a beautiful pea-green boat,
They took some honey, and plenty of money;
Wrapped up in a five-pound note.
The Owl looked up to the stars above,
And sang to a small guitar,
"O lovely Pussy, O Pussy my love,
What a beautiful Pussy you are,
    You are,
    You are!
What a beautiful Pussy you are!"

Pussy said to the Owl, "You elegant fowl!
How charmingly sweet you sing!
O let us be married! Too long we have tarried:
But what shall we do for a ring?"
They sailed away for a year and a day,
To the land where the Bong-tree grows,
And there in a wood a Piggy-wig stood,
With a ring at the end of his nose,
   His nose,
   His nose,
With a ring at the end of his nose.

"Dear Pig, are you willing to sell for one shilling
Your ring?" Said the Piggy, "I will."
So they took it away, and were married next day
By the Turkey who lives on the hill.
They dined on mince, and slices of quince,
Which they ate with a runcible spoon;
And hand in hand, on the edge of the sand,
They danced by the light of the moon,
   The moon,
   The moon,
They danced by the light of the moon.

Edward Lear

Jabberwocky

'Twas brillig, and the slithy toves
Did gyre and gimble in the wabe:
All mimsy were the borogoves,
And the mome raths outgrabe.

"Beware the Jabberwock, my son!
The jaws that bite, the claws that catch!
Beware the Jubjub bird, and shun
The frumious Bandersnatch!"

He took his vorpal sword in hand:
Long time the manxome foe he sought –
So rested he by the Tumtum tree,
And stood awhile in thought.

And, as in uffish thought he stood,
The Jabberwock, with eyes of flame,
Came whiffling through the tulgey wood,
And burbled as it came!

One, two! One, two! And through and through
The vorpal blade went snicker-snack!
He left it dead, and with its head
He went galumphing back.

"And hast thou slain the Jabberwock?
Come to my arms, my beamish boy!
O frabjous day! Callooh! Callay!"
He chortled in his joy.

'Twas brillig, and the slithy toves
Did gyre and gimble in the wabe:
All mimsy were the borogoves,
And the mome raths outgrabe.

Lewis Carroll

Hurt No Living Thing

Hurt no living thing;
Ladybird, nor butterfly,
Nor moth with dusty wing,
Nor cricket chirping cheerily,
Nor grasshopper so light of leap,
Nor dancing gnat, nor beetle fat,
Nor harmless worms that creep.

Christina Rossetti

How Doth the Little Crocodile

How doth the little crocodile
Improve his shining tail;
And pour the waters of the Nile
On every golden scale!

How cheerfully he seems to grin,
How neatly spreads his claws,
And welcomes little fishes in,
With gently smiling jaws!

Lewis Carroll

Auguries of Innocence

To see a World in a Grain of Sand
And a Heaven in a Wild Flower,
Hold Infinity in the palm of your hand
And Eternity in an hour.

A Robin Red breast in a Cage
Puts all Heaven in a Rage.
A dove house fill'd with doves & Pigeons
Shudders Hell thro' all its regions.
A dog starv'd at his Master's Gate
Predicts the ruin of the State.
A Horse misus'd upon the Road
Calls to Heaven for Human blood.

Each outcry of the hunted Hare
A fiber from the Brain does tear.
A Skylark wounded in the wing,
A Cherubim does cease to sing.
The Game Cock clip'd & arm'd for fight
Does the Rising Sun affright.
Every Wolf's & Lion's howl
Raises from Hell a Human Soul.
The wild deer, wand'ring here & there,
Keeps the Human Soul from Care.
The Lamb misus'd breeds Public strife
And yet forgives the Butcher's Knife.
The Bat that flits at close of Eve
Has left the Brain that won't Believe.
The Owl that calls upon the Night
Speaks the Unbeliever's fright.
He who shall hurt the little Wren
Shall never be belov'd by Men.
He who the Ox to wrath has mov'd
Shall never be by Woman lov'd.
The wanton Boy that kills the Fly
Shall fell the Spider's enmity.
He who torments the Chafer's sprite
Weaves a Bower in endless Night.
The Catterpiller on the Leaf
Repeats to thee thy Mother's grief.
Kill not the Moth nor Butterfly,
For the Last Judgment draweth nigh.

William Blake

The Herring Loves
the Merry Moonlight

The herring loves the merry moonlight,
The mackerel loves the wind,
But the oyster loves the dredging sang,
For they come of a gentle kind.

Sir Walter Scott

The Maldive Shark

About the Shark, phlegmatical one,
Pale sot of the Maldive sea,
The sleek little pilot-fish, azure and slim,
How alert in attendance be.
From his saw-pit of mouth, from his charnel of maw
They have nothing of harm to dread,
But liquidly glide on his ghastly flank
Or before his Gorgonian head;
Or luck in the port of serrated teeth
In white triple tiers of glittering gates,
And there find a haven when peril's abroad,
An asylum in jaws of the Fates!
They are friends; and friendly they guide him to prey,
Yet never partake of the treat –
Eyes and brains to the dotard lethargic and dull,
Pale ravener of horrible meat.

Herman Melville

My Cat Jeoffry

For I will consider my cat Jeoffry.
For he is the servant of the Living God,
    duly and daily serving him.
For at the first glance of the glory of God in the
    East he worships in his way.
For is this done by wreathing his body seven times
    round with elegant quickness.
For then he leaps up to catch the musk,
    which is the blessing of God upon his prayer.
For he rolls upon prank to work it in.
For having done duty and received blessing he
    begins to consider himself.
For this he performs in ten degrees.
For first he looks upon his fore-paws to see if
    they are clean.
For secondly he kicks up behind to clear away
    there.
For thirdly he works it upon stretch with the
    fore-paws extended.
For fourthly he sharpens his paws by wood.
For fifthly he washes himself.
For sixthly he rolls upon wash.
For seventhly he fleas himself, that he may
    not be interrupted upon the beat.
For eighthly he rubs himself against a post.
For ninthly he looks up for his instructions.
For tenthly he goes in quest of food.
For having considered God and himself he
    will consider his neighbor.

For if he meets another cat he will kiss her in
kindness.
For when he takes his prey he plays with it to
give it chance.
For one mouse in seven escapes by his dallying.
For when his day's work is done his business
more properly begins.
For he keeps the Lord's watch in the night
against the adversary.
For he counteracts the powers of darkness by his
electrical skin & glaring eyes.
For he counteracts the Devil, who is death, by
brisking about the life.
For in his morning orisons he loves the sun
and the sun loves him.
For he is of the tribe of Tiger.
For the Cherub Cat is a term of the Angel Tiger.
For he has the subtlety and hissing of a serpent,
which in goodness he suppresses.
For he will not do destruction, if he is well-fed,
neither will he spit without provocation.
For he purrs in thankfulness, when God tells
him he's a good Cat.
For he is an instrument for the children to learn
benevolence upon.
For every house is incompleat without him and
a blessing is lacking in the spirit.

Christopher Smart

The Owl

When cats run home and light is come,
And dew is cold upon the ground,
And the far-off stream is dumb,
And the whirring sail goes round,
And the whirring sail goes round;
Alone and warming his five wits,
The white owl in the belfry sits.

When merry milkmaids click the latch,
And rarely smells the new-mown hay,
And the cock hath sung beneath the thatch
Twice or thrice his roundelay,
Twice or thrice his roundelay;
Alone and warming his five wits
The white owl in the belfry sits.

Alfred, Lord Tennyson

The Silver Swan

The silver swan, who living had no note,
When death approached, unlocked her silent throat,
Leaning her breast against the reedy shore,
Thus sung her first and last, and sung no more:
Farewell all joys! O death, come close mine eyes;
More geese than swans now live, more fools than wise.

Anonymous

The Tyger

Tyger! Tyger! burning bright
In the forests of the night,
What immortal hand or eye
Could frame thy fearful symmetry?

In what distant deeps or skies
Burnt the fire of thine eyes?
On what wings dare he aspire?
What the hand dare seize the fire?

And what shoulder, & what art,
Could twist the sinews of thy heart?
And when thy heart began to beat,
What dread hand? & what dread feet?

What the hammer? what the chain?
In what furnace was thy brain?
What the anvil? what dread grasp
Dare its deadly terrors clasp?

When the stars threw down their spears,
And water'd heaven with their tears,
Did he smile his work to see?
Did he who make the Lamb make thee?

Tyger! Tyger! burning bright
In the forests of the night,
What immortal hand or eye
Could frame thy fearful symmetry?

William Blake

The Eagle

He clasps the crag with crooked hands;
Close to the sun in lonely lands,
Ring'd with the azure world, he stands.

The wrinkled sea beneath him crawls;
He watches from his mountain walls,
And like a thunderbolt he falls.

Alfred, Lord Tennyson

WEATHER
and
SEASONS

Whether the Weather Be Fine

Whether the weather be fine
Or whether the weather be not,
Whether the weather be cold
Or whether the weather be hot,
We'll weather the weather
Whatever the weather,
Whether we like it or not.

Anonymous

It's Raining, It's Pouring

It's raining, it's pouring,
The old man is snoring;
He went to bed and bumped his head
And couldn't get up in the morning!

Anonymous

The Rainbow

Boats sail on the rivers,
And ships sail on the seas;
But clouds that sail across the sky
Are prettier far than these.

These are bridges on the rivers,
As pretty as you please;
But the bow that bridges heaven,
And overtops the trees,
And builds a road from earth to sky,
Is prettier far than these.

Christina Rossetti

The Wind

Who has seen the wind?
Neither I nor you;
But when the leaves hang trembling
The wind is passing through.

Who has seen the wind?
Neither you nor I;
But when the trees bow down their heads
The wind is passing by.

Christina Rossetti

The North Wind Doth Blow

The north wind doth blow,
And we shall have snow,
And what will poor robin do then,
Poor thing?

He'll sit in a barn,
And keep himself warm,
And hide his head under his wing,
Poor thing.

Anonymous

Windy Nights

Whenever the moon and stars are set,
Whenever the wind is high,
All night long in the dark and wet,
A man goes riding by.
Late in the night when the fires are out,
Why does he gallop and gallop about?

Whenever the trees are crying aloud,
And ships are tossed at sea,
By, on the highway, low and loud,
By at the gallop goes he.
By at the gallop he goes, and then
By he comes back at the gallop again.

Robert Louis Stevenson

The Human Seasons

Four seasons fill the measure of the year;
There are four seasons in the mind of man:
He has his lusty Spring, when fancy clear
Takes in all beauty with an easy span:

He has his Summer, when luxuriously
Spring's honey'd cud of youthful thought he loves
To ruminate, and by such dreaming nigh
His nearest unto heaven: quiet coves

His soul has in its Autumn, when his wings
He furleth close; contented so to look
On mists in idleness – to let fair things
Pass by unheeded as a threshold brook:

He has his Winter too of pale misfeature,
Or else he would forgo his mortal nature.

John Keats

Winter

When icicles hang by the wall,
And Dick the shepherd blows his nail,
And Tom bears logs into the hall,
And milk comes frozen home in pail;
When blood is nipped, and ways be foul,
Then nightly sings the staring owl.
Tu-whit, tu-who! a merry note,
While greasy Joan doth keep the pot.

When all aloud the wind doth blow,
And coughing drowns the parson's saw,
And birds sit brooding in the snow,
And Marian's nose looks red and raw,
When roasted crabs hiss in the bowl,
Then nightly sings the staring owl,
Tu-whit, tu-who! a merry note,
When greasy Joan doth keel the pot.

William Shakespeare

Spring

Sound the Flute!
Now it's mute.
Birds delight
Day and Night;
Nightingale
In the dale,
Lark in Sky,
Merrily,
Merrily, Merrily, to welcome in the Year.

Little Boy,
Full of joy;
Little Girl,
Sweet and small,
Cock does crow,
So do you;
Merry voice,
Infant noise,
Merrily, Merrily, to welcome in the Year.

Little Lamb,
Here I am;
Come and lick
My white neck;
Let me pull
Your soft Wool;
Let me kiss
Your soft face:
Merrily, Merrily, we welcome in the Year.

William Blake

From Rain in Summer

How beautiful is the rain!
After the dust and heat,
In the broad and fiery street,
In the narrow lane,
How beautiful is the rain!

How it clatters along the roofs,
Like the tramp of hoofs!
How it gushes and struggles out
From the throat of the overflowing spout!

Across the window-pane
It pours and pours;
And swift and wide,
With a muddy tide,
Live a river down the gutter roars
The rain, the welcome rain!

Henry Wadsworth Longfellow

Fall, Leaves, Fall

Fall, leaves, fall: die, flowers, away;
Lengthen night and shorten day,
Every leaf speaks bliss to me
Fluttering from the autumn tree.
I shall smile when wreaths of snow
Blossom where the rose should grow;
I shall sing when night's decay
Ushers in a drearier day.

Emily Brontë

The Year's at the Spring

The year's at the spring
And day's at the morn;
Morning's at seven;
The hill-side's dew-pearled;
The lark's on the wing;
The snail's on the thorn:
God's in his heaven –
All's right with the world!

Robert Browning

BRIGHT
and
BEAUTIFUL

Pied Beauty

Glory be to God for dappled things –
For skies of couple-color as a brinded cow;
For rose-moles all in stipple upon trout that swim;
Fresh-firecoal chestnut-falls; finches' wings;
Landscape plotted and pieced – fold, fallow, and plough;
And all trades, their gear and tackle and trim.

All things counter, original, spare, strange;
Whatever is fickle, freckled (who knows how?)
With swift, slow; sweet, sour; adazzle, dim;
He fathers-forth whose beauty is past change:
Praise him

Gerard Manley Hopkins

My Shadow

I have a little shadow that goes in and out with me,
And what can be the use of him is more than I can see.
His is very, very like me from the heels up to the head;
And I see him jump before me, when I jump into my bed.

The funniest thing about him is the way he likes to grow –
Not at all like proper children, which is always very slow;
For he sometimes shoots up taller like an india-rubber ball,
And he sometimes gets so little that there's none of him at all.

He hasn't got a notion of how children ought to play,
And can only make a fool of me in every sort of way.
He stays so close behind me he's a coward you can see;
I'd think shame to stick to nursie as that shadow sticks to me!

One morning, very early, before the sun was up,
I rose and found the shining dew on every buttercup;
But my lazy little shadow, like an arrant sleepy-head,
Had stayed at home behind me and was fast asleep in bed.

Robert Louis Stevenson

Daffodils

I wandered lonely as a cloud
        That floats on high o'er vales and hills,
When all at once I saw a crowd,
        A host, of golden daffodils;
Beside the lake, beneath the trees,
Fluttering and dancing in the breeze.

Continuous as the stars that shine
    And twinkle on the Milky Way,
They stretched in never-ending line
    Along the margin of a bay:
Ten thousand saw I at a glance,
Tossing their heads in sprightly dance.

The waves beside them danced, but they
    Out-did the sparkling waves in glee:
A poet could not but be gay,
    In such a jocund company:
I gazed – and gazed – but little thought
What wealth the show to me had brought:

For oft, when on my couch I lie
    In vacant or in pensive mood,
They flash upon that inward eye
    Which is the bliss of solitude;
And then my heart with pleasure fills,
And dances with the daffodils.

William Wordsworth

The Echoing Green

The sun does arise;
And make happy the skies.
The merry bells ring
To welcome the Spring;
The skylark and thrush,
The birds of the bush,
Sing louder around
To the bells' chearful sound,
While our sports shall be seen
On the Echoing Green.

Old John, with white hair,
Does laugh away care,
Sitting under the oak,
Among the old folk.
They laugh at our play,
And soon they all say:
"Such, such were the joys
When we were all, girls and boys,
In our youth time were seen
On the Echoing Green."

Till the little ones, weary,
No more can be merry;
The sun does descend,
And our sports have an end.
Round the laps of their mothers
Many sisters and brothers,
Like birds in their nest,
Are ready for rest,
And sport no more seen
On the darkening Green.

William Blake

She Walks in Beauty

She walks in beauty, like the night
    Of cloudless climes and starry skies;
And all that's best of dark and bright
    Meet in her aspect and her eyes:
Thus mellowed to that tender light
    Which heaven to gaudy day denies.

One shade the more, one ray the less,
    Had half impaired the nameless grace
Which waves in every raven tress,
    Or softly lightens o'er her face;
Where thoughts serenely sweet express
    How pure, how dear their dwelling-place.

And on that cheek, and o'er that brow,
    So soft, so calm, yet eloquent,
The smiles that win, the tints that glow,
    But tell of days in goodness spent,
A mind at peace with all below,
    A heart whose love is innocent!

George Gordon, Lord Byron

Shall I Compare Thee to a Summer's Day?

Shall I compare thee to a summer's day?
>Thou art more lovely and more temperate:
Rough winds do shake the darling buds of May,
>And Summer's lease hath all too short a date:
Sometime too hot the eye of heaven shines,
>And often is his gold complexion dimmed;
And every fair from fair sometime declines,
>By chance, or nature's changing course untrimmed;
But thy eternal summer shall not fade,
>Nor lose possession of that fair thou owest,
Nor shall Death brag thou wanderest in his shade,
>When in eternal lines to time thou growest;
So long as men can breathe, or eyes can see,
So long lives this, and this gives life to thee.

William Shakespeare

Blow, Bugle, Blow

The splendour falls on castle walls
    And snowy summits old in story:
The long light shakes across the lakes,
    And the wild cataract leaps in glory.
Blow, bugle, blow, set the wild echoes flying,
Blow, bugle; answer, echoes, dying, dying, dying.

O hark, O hear! how thin and clear,
    And thinner, clearer, farther going!
O sweet and far from cliff and scar
    The horns of Elfland faintly blowing!
Blow, let us hear the purple glens replying:
Blow, bugle; answer, echoes, dying, dying, dying.

O love, they die in yon rich sky,
    They faint on hill or field or river:
Our echoes roll from soul to soul,
    And grow for ever and for ever.
Blow, bugle, blow, set the wild echoes flying,
And answer, echoes, answer, dying, dying, dying.

Alfred, Lord Tennyson

DREAMS
and
WONDERS

Kubla Khan

In Xanadu did Kubla Khan
  A stately pleasure-dome decree:
Where Alph, the sacred river, ran
Through caverns measureless to man
  Down to a sunless sea.
So twice five miles of fertile ground
  With walls and towers were girdled round:
And there were gardens bright with sinuous rills
Where blossomed many an incense-bearing tree;
And here were forests ancient as the hills,
Enfolding sunny spots of greenery.

But O, that deep romantic chasm which slanted
Down the green hill athwart a cedarn cover!
A savage place! as holy and enchanted
As e'er beneath a waning moon was haunted
By woman wailing for her demon-lover!
And from this chasm, with ceaseless turmoil seething,
As if this earth in fast thick pants were breathing,
A mighty fountain momently was forced;
Amid whose swift half-intermitted burst
Huge fragments vaulted like rebounding hail,
Or chaffy grain beneath the thresher's flail:
And 'mid these dancing rocks at once and ever
It flung up momently the sacred river.
Five miles meandering with a mazy motion
Through wood and dale the sacred river ran,
Then reached the caverns measureless to man,
And sank in tumult to a lifeless ocean:
And 'mid this tumult Kubla heard from far
Ancestral voices prophesying war!

    The shadow of the dome of pleasure
        Floated midway on the waves;
    Where was heard the mingled measure
        From the fountain and the caves.
    It was a miracle of rare device,
    A sunny pleasure-dome with caves of ice!

A damsel with a dulcimer
    In a vision once I saw:
It was an Abyssinian maid,
    And on her dulcimer she played,
Singing of Mount Abora.
Could I revive within me,
    Her symphony and song,
To such a deep delight 'twould win me,
That with music loud and long,
I would build that dome in air,
That sunny dome! those caves of ice!
And all who heard should see them there,
And all should cry, Beware! Beware!
His flashing eyes, his floating hair!
    Weave a circle round him thrice,
    And close your eyes with holy dread,
For he on honey-dew hath fed,
    And drunk the milk of Paradise.

Samuel Taylor Coleridge

The Fairies

Up the airy mountain,
Down the rushy glen,
We daren't go a-hunting
For fear of little men;
Wee folk, good folk,
Trooping all together;
Green jacket, red cap,
And white owl's feather!

Down along the rocky shore
Some make their home,
They live on crispy pancakes
Of yellow tide-foam;
Some in the reeds
Of the black mountain-lake,
With frogs for their watch-dogs,
All night awake.

High on the hill-top
The old King sits;
He is now so old and gray
He's right lost his wits.
With a bridge of white mist
Columbkill he crosses,
On his stately journeys
From Slieveleague to Rosses;
Or going up with music
On cold starry nights,
To sup with the Queen
Of the gay Northern Lights.

They stole little Bridget
For seven years long;
When she came down again
Her friends were all gone.
They took her lightly back,
Between the night and morrow,
They thought she was fast asleep,
But she was dead with sorrow.
They have kept her ever since
Deep within the lake,
On a bed of flag-leaves,
Watching till she wake.

By the craggy hill-side,
Through the mosses bare,
They have planted thorn-trees
For pleasure here and there.
Is any man so daring
As dig them up in spite,
He shall find the sharpest thorns
In his bed at night.

Up the airy mountain,
Down the rushy glen,
We daren't go a-hunting
For fear of little men;
Wee folk, good folk,
Trooping all together;
Green jacket, red cap,
And white owl's feather!

William Allingham

La Belle Dame Sans Merci

O what can ail thee, knight-at-arms,
Alone and palely loitering?
The sedge has wither'd from the lake,
And no birds sing.

O what can ail thee, knight-at-arms,
So haggard and so woe-begone?
The squirrel's granary is full,
And the harvest's done.

I see a lily on thy brow,
With anguish moist and fever dew;
And on thy cheeks a fading rose
Fast withereth too.

I met a lady in the meads,
Full beautiful – a faery's child,
Her hair was long, her foot was light,
And her eyes were wild.

I made a garland for her head,
And bracelets too, and fragrant zone;
She look'd at me as she did love,
And made sweet moan.

I set her on my pacing steed,
And nothing else saw all day long;
For sidelong would she bend, and sing
A faery's song.

She found me roots of relish sweet,
And honey wild, and manna dew,
And sure in language strange she said –
"I love thee true".

She took me to her elfin grot,
And there she wept, and sigh'd full sore,
And there I shut her wild wild eyes
With kisses four.

And there she lulled me asleep
And there I dream'd – Ah! woe betide!
The latest dream I ever dream'd
On the cold hill's side.

I saw pale kings and princes too,
Pale warriors, death-pale were they all;
They cried – "La Belle Dame sans Merci
Hath thee in thrall!"

I saw their starved lips in the gloam,
With horrid warning gaped wide,
And I awoke and found me here,
On the cold hill's side.

And this is why I sojourn here
Alone and palely loitering,
Though the sedge is wither'd from the lake,
And no birds sing.

John Keats

I Saw a Peacock

I saw a peacock with a fiery tail
I saw a blazing comet drop down hail
I saw a cloud wrapped with ivy round,
I an oak creep upon the ground
I saw a pismire swallow up a whale
I saw the sea brimful of ale
I saw a Venice glass full fifteen feet deep
I saw a well full of men's tears that weep
I saw red eyes all of a flaming fire
I saw a house bigger than the moon and higher
I saw the sun at twelve o'clock at night
I saw the man that saw this wondrous sight.

Anonymous

A Child's Thought

At seven, when I go to bed,
I find such pictures in my head:
Castles with dragons prowling round,
Gardens with magic fruits are found;
Fair ladies prisoned in a tower,
Or lost in an enchanted bower;
While gallant horsemen ride by streams
That border all this land of dreams
I find, so clearly in my head
At seven, when I go to bed.

Robert Louis Stevenson

SONGS
of
THE SEA

Full Fathom Five

Full fathom five thy father lies;
Of his bones are coral made;
Those are pearls that were his eyes:
Nothing of him that doth fade,
But doth suffer a sea–change
Into something rich and strange:
Sea nymphs hourly ring his knell.
        Ding–dong!
Hark! now I hear them,
            Ding–dong, bell!

William Shakespeare

What Are Heavy?

What are heavy? Sea–sand and sorrow:
What are brief? Today and tomorrow:
What are frail? Spring blossoms and youth:
What are deep? The ocean and truth.

Christina Rossetti

I Started Early

I started Early – Took my Dog –
And visited the Sea –
The Mermaids in the Basement
Came out to look at me –

And Frigates – in the Upper Floor
Extended Hempen Hands –
Presuming Me to be a Mouse –
Aground – upon the Sands –

But no Man moved Me – till the Tide
Went past my simple Shoe –
And past my Apron – and my Belt
And past my Bodice – too –

And made as He would eat me up –
As wholly as a Dew
Upon a Dandelion's Sleeve –
And then – I started – too –

And He – He followed – close behind –
I felt His Silver Heel
Upon my Ankle – Then my Shoes
Would overflow with Pearl –

Until We met the Solid Town –
No One He seemed to know –
And bowing – with a Mighty look –
At me – The Sea withdrew –

Emily Dickinson

O Captain! My Captain!

O Captain! my Captain! our fearful trip is done,
The ship has weather'd every rack, the prize we sought is won,
The port is near, the bells I hear, the people all exulting,
While follow eyes the steady keel, the vessel grim and daring;
    But O heart! heart! heart!
    O the bleeding drops of red,
    Where on the deck my Captain lies,
    Fallen cold and dead.

O Captain! my Captain! rise up and hear the bells;
Rise up – for you the flag is flung – for you the bugle trills,
For you bouquets and ribbon'd wreaths – for you the shores a-crowding,
For you they call, the swaying mass, their eager faces turning;
Here Captain! dear father!
This arm beneath your head!
It is some dream that on the deck,
You've fallen cold and dead.

My Captain does not answer, his lips are pale and still,
My father does not feel my arm, he has no pulse nor will,
The ship is anchor'd safe and sound, its voyage closed and done,
From fearful trip, the victor ship, comes in with object won;
Exult O shores, and ring O bells!
But I with mournful tread,
Walk the deck my Captain lies,
Fallen cold and dead.

Walt Whitman

Break, Break, Break

Break, break, break,
    On thy cold grey stones, O Sea!
And I would that my tongue could utter
    The thoughts that arise in me.

O, well for the fisherman's boy,
    That he shouts with his sister at play!
O, well for the sailor lad,
    That he sings in his boat on the bay!

And the stately ships go on
    To their haven under the hill;
But O for the touch of a vanish'd hand,
    And the sound of a voice that is still!

Break, break, break,
    At the foot of thy crags, O sea!
But the tender grace of a day that is dead
    Will never come back to me.

Alfred, Lord Tennyson

Meeting at Night

The grey sea and the long black land;
And the yellow half-moon large and low;
And the startled little waves that leap
In fiery ringlets from their sleep,
As I gain the cove with pushing prow,
And quench its speed i' the slushy sand.

Then a mile of warm sea-scented beach;
Three fields to cross till a farm appears;
A tap at the pane, the quick sharp scratch
And blue spurt of a lighted match,
And a voice less loud, thro' its joys and fears,
Than the two hearts beating each to each!

Robert Browning

TALES
of
TRAVEL

Ozymandias

I met a traveller from an antique land
Who said: Two vast and trunkless legs of stone
Stand in the desert ... Near them, on the sand,
Half sunk, a shattered visage lies, whose frown,
And wrinkled lip, and sneer of cold command,
Tell that its sculptor well those passions read
Which yet survive, stamped on these lifeless things,
The hand that mocked them, and the heart that fed:
And on the pedestal these words appear:
"My name is Ozymandias, king of kings:
Look on my works, ye Mighty, and despair!"
Nothing beside remains. Round the decay
Of that colossal wreck, boundless and bare
The lone and level sands stretch far away.

Percy Bysshe Shelley

Where Lies the Land?

Where lies the land to which the ship would go?
Far, far ahead, is all her seamen know.
And where the land she travels from? Away,
Far, far behind, is all that they can say.

On sunny noons upon the deck's smooth face,
Linked arm in arm, how pleasant here to pace;
Or, o'er the stern reclining, watch below
The foaming wake far widening as we go.

On stormy nights when wild north-westers rave,
How proud a thing to fight with wind and wave!
The dripping sailor on the reeling mast
Exults to bear, and scorns to wish it past.

Where lies the land to which the ship would go?
Far, far ahead, is all her seamen know.
And where the land she travels from? Away,
Far, far behind, is all that they can say.

Arthur Hugh Clough

Eldorado

Gaily bedight,
A gallant knight,
In sunshine and in shadow,
Had journeyed long,
Singing a song,
In search of Eldorado.

But he grew old –
This knight so bold –
And o'er his heart a shadow
Fell, as he found
No spot of ground
That looked like Eldorado.

And, as his strength
Failed him at length,
He met a pilgrim shadow –
"Shadow," said he,
"Where can it be –
This land of Eldorado?"

"Over the Mountains
Of the Moon,
Down the Valley of the Shadow,
Ride, boldly ride,"
The shade replied,
"If you seek for Eldorado!"

Edgar Allen Poe

Foreign Lands

Up into the cherry-tree
Who should climb but little me?
I held the trunk with both my hands
And looked abroad on foreign lands.

I saw the next-door garden lie,
Adorned with flowers, before my eye,
And many pleasant places more
That I had never seen before.

I saw the dimpling river pass
And be the sky's blue looking-glass;
The dusty roads go up and down
With people tramping in to town.

If I could find a higher tree
Farther and farther I should see,
To where the grown-up river slips
Into the sea among the ships,

To where the roads on either hand
Lead onward into fairy land,
Where all the children dine at five,
And all the playthings come alive.

Robert Louis Stevenson

Uphill

Does the road wind uphill all the way?
Yes, to the very end.
Will the day's journey take the whole long day?
From morn to night, my friend.

But is there for the night a resting-place?
A roof for when the slow, dark hours begin.
May not the darkness hide it from my face?
You cannot miss that inn.

Shall I meet other wayfarers at night?
Those who have gone before.
Then must I knock, or call when just in sight?
They will not keep you waiting at that door.

Shall I find comfort, travel-sore and weak?
Of labour you shall find the sum.
Will there be beds for me and all who seek?
Yea, beds for all who come.

Christina Rossetti

Travel

I should like to rise and go
Where the golden apples grow;
Where below another sky
Parrot islands anchored lie,
And, watched by cockatoos and goats,
Lonely Crusoes building boats;
Where in sunshine reaching out
Eastern cities, miles about,
Are with mosque and minaret
Among sandy gardens set,
And the rich goods from near and far
Hang for sale in the bazaar;
Where the Great Wall round China goes,
And on one side the desert blows,
And with bell and voice and drum,
Cities on the other hum;

Where are forests, hot as fire,
Wide as England, tall as a spire,
Full of apes and coco-nuts
And the negro hunters' huts;
Where the knotty crocodile
Lies and blinks in the Nile,
And the red flamingo flies
Hunting fish before his eyes;

Where in jungles, near and far,
Man-devouring tigers are,
Lying close and giving ear
Lest the hunt be drawing near,
Or a comer-by be seen
Swinging in a palanquin;
Where among the desert sands
Some deserted city stands,

All its children, sweep and prince,
Grown to manhood ages since,
Not a foot in street or house,
Not a stir of child or mouse,
And when kindly falls the night,
In all the town no spark of light.
There I'll come when I'm a man
With a camel caravan;
Light a fire in the gloom
Of some dusty dining-room;
See the pictures on the walls,
Heroes, fights and festivals;
And in a corner find the toys
Of the old Egyptian boys.

Robert Louis Stevenson

From a Railway Carriage

Faster than fairies, faster than witches,
Bridges and houses, hedges and ditches;
And charging along like troops in a battle,
All through the meadows, the horses and cattle:
All of the sights of the hill and the plain
Fly as thick as driving rain;
And ever again, in the wink of an eye,
Painted stations whistle by.

Here is a child who clambers and scrambles,
All by himself and gathering brambles;
Here is a tramp who stands and gazes;
And there is the green for stringing the daisies!
Here is a cart run away on the road
Lumping along with man and load;
And here is a mill and there is a river:
Each a glimpse and gone for ever!

Robert Louis Stevenson

CHILDHOOD

Little Orphant Annie

Little Orphant Annie's come to our house to stay,
An' wash the cups an' saucers up, an' brush the crumbs away,
An' shoo the chickens off the porch, an' dust the hearth, an' sweep,
An' make the fire, an' bake the bread, an' earn her board-an'-keep;
An' all us other childern, when the supper-things is done,
We set around the kitchen fire an' has the mostest fun
A-list'nin' to the witch-tales 'at Annie tells about,
An' the Gobble-uns at 'gits you
  Ef you
   Don't
    Watch
     Out!

Wunst they wuz a little boy wouldn't say his prayers,–
An' when he went to bed at night, away up-stairs,
His Mammy heerd him holler, an' his Daddy heerd him bawl,
An' when they turn't the kivvers down, he wuzn't there at all!
An' they seeked him in the rafter-room, an' cubby-hole, an' press,
An' seeked him up the chimbly-flue, an' ever'wheres, I guess;
But all they ever found wuz thist his pants an' roundabout:–
An' the Gobble-uns 'll git you
  Ef you
   Don't
    Watch
     Out!

An' one time a little girl 'ud allus laugh an' grin,
An' make fun of ever' one, an' all her blood-an'-kin;
An' wunst, when they was "company," an' ole folks wuz there,
She mocked 'em an' shocked 'em, an' said she didn't care!
An' thist as she kicked her heels, an' turn't to run an' hide,
They wuz two great big Black Things a-standin' by her side,
An' they snatched her through the ceilin' 'fore she knowed what she's about!
An' the Gobble-uns 'll git you
    Ef you
        Don't
            Watch
                Out!

An' little Orphant Annie says, when the blaze is blue,
An' the lamp-wick sputters, an' the wind goes woo-oo!
An' you hear the crickets quit, an' the moon is gray,
An' the lightnin'-bugs in dew is all squenched away,–
You better mind yer parunts, an' yer teachurs fond an' dear,
An' churish them 'at loves you, an' dry the orphant's tear,
An' he'p the pore an' needy ones 'at clusters all about,
Er the Gobble-uns 'll git you
    Ef you
        Don't
            Watch
                Out!

James Whitcomb Riley

Monday's Child

Monday's child is fair of face,
Tuesday's child is full of grace,
Wednesday's child is full of woe,
Thursday's child has far to go,
Friday's child is loving and giving,
Saturday's child works hard for his living,
And the child that is born on the Sabbath day
Is bonny and blithe, and good and gay.

Anonymous

A Child's Grace

Here a little child I stand
Heaving up my either hand;
Cold as paddocks though they be,
Here I lift them up to Thee,
For a benison to fall
On our meat and on us all.
Amen.

Robert Herrick

I Remember, I Remember

I remember, I remember,
The house where I was born,
The little window where the sun
Came peeping in at morn;
He never came a wink too soon,
Nor brought too long a day,
But now, I often wish the night
Had borne my breath away!

I remember, I remember,
The roses, red and white,
The violets and the lily-cups,
Those flowers made of light!
The lilacs where the robin built,
And where my brother set
The laburnum on his birthday,–
The tree is living yet!

I remember, I remember,
Where I was used to swing,
And thought the air must rush as fresh
To swallows on the wing;
My spirit flew in feathers then,
That is so heavy now,
The summer pools could hardly cool
The fever on my brow!

I remember, I remember,
The fir-trees dark and high;
I used to think their slender tops
Were close against the sky:
It was a childish ignorance,
But now 'tis little joy
To know I'm farther off from Heaven
Than when I was a boy.

Thomas Hood

Swing, Swing

Swing, swing,
Sing, sing,
Here! my throne and I am a king!
Swing, sing,
Sing, sing,
Farewell, earth, for I'm on the wing!

Low, high,
Here I fly,
Like a bird through sunny sky;
Free, free,
Over the lea,
Over the mountain, over the sea!

Soon, soon,
Afternoon,
Over the sunset, over the moon;
Far, far,
Over all bar,
Sweeping on from star to star!

No, no,
Low, low,
Sweeping daisies with my toe.
Slow, slow,
To and fro,
Slow – slow – slow – slow.

William Allingham

Good and Bad Children

Children, you are very little,
And your bones are very brittle;
If you would grow great and stately,
You must try to walk sedately.

You must still be bright and quiet,
And content with simple diet;
And remain, through all bewild'ring,
Innocent and honest children.

Happy hearts and happy faces,
Happy play in grassy places –
That was how, in ancient ages,
Children grew to kings and sages.

But the unkind and the unruly,
And the sort who eat unduly,
They must never hope for glory –
Theirs is quite a different story!

Cruel children, crying babies,
All grow up as geese and gabies,
Hated, as their age increases,
By their nephews and their nieces.

Robert Louis Stevenson

AT THE END
of
THE DAY

Escape at Bedtime

The lights from the parlour and kitchen shone out
 Through the blinds and the windows and bars;
And high overhead and all moving about,
 There were thousands of millions of stars.
There ne'er were such thousands of leaves on a tree,
 Nor of people in church or the Park,
As the crowds of the stars that looked down upon me,
 And that glittered and winked in the dark.

The Dog, and the Plough, and the Hunter, and all,
 And the star of the sailor, and Mars,
These shown in the sky, and the pail by the wall
 Would be half full of water and stars.
They saw me at last, and they chased me with cries,
 And they soon had me packed into bed;
But the glory kept shining and bright in my eyes,
 And the stars going round in my head.

Robert Louis Stevenson

Bed in Summer

In winter I get up at night
And dress by yellow candle-light.
In summer quite the other way,
I have to go to bed by day.

I have to go to bed and see
The birds still hopping on the tree,
Or hear the grown-up people's feet
Still going past me in the street.

And does it not seem hard to you,
When all the sky is clear and blue,
And I should like so much to play,
To have to go to bed by day?

Robert Louis Stevenson

Is The Moon Tired?

Is the moon tired? She looks so pale
        Within her misty veil;
She scales the sky from east to west,
        And takes no rest.

Before the coming of the night
        The moon shows papery white;
Before the dawning of the day
        She fades away.

Christina Rossetti

Wynken, Blynken, and Nod

Wynken, Blynken, and Nod one night
Sailed off in a wooden shoe –
Sailed on a river of crystal light,
Into a sea of dew.
"Where are you going, and what do you wish?"
The old moon asked the three.
"We have come to fish for the herring fish
That live in this beautiful sea;
Nets of silver and gold have we!"
      Said Wynken,
      Blynken,
      And Nod.

The old moon laughed and sang a song,
As they rocked in the wooden shoe,
And the wind that sped them all night long
Ruffled the waves of dew.
The little stars were the herring fish
That lived in that beautiful sea –
"Now cast your nets wherever you wish –
Never afeard are we";
So cried the stars to the fishermen three:
      Wynken,
      Blynken,
      And Nod.

All night long their nets they threw
To the stars in the twinkling foam –
Then down from the skies came the wooden shoe,
Bringing the fishermen home;
'T was all so pretty a sail it seemed
As if it could not be,
And some folks thought 'twas a dream they'd
dreamed
Of sailing that beautiful sea –
But I shall name you the fishermen three:
  Wynken,
  Blynken,
  And Nod.

Wynken and Blynken are two little eyes,
And Nod is a little head,
And the wooden shoe that sailed the skies
Is a wee one's trundle-bed.
So shut your eyes while mother sings
Of wonderful sights that be,
And you shall see the beautiful things
As you rock in the misty sea,
Where the old shoe rocked the fishermen three:
  Wynken,
  Blynken,
  And Nod.

Eugene Field

How Many Miles to Babylon?

How many miles to Babylon?
Three score miles and ten.
Can I get there by candlelight?
Yes, and back again.
If your heels are nimble and light,
You may get there by candlelight.

Anonymous

Star Light, Star Bright

Star light, star bright,
First star I see tonight,
I wish I may, I wish I might,
Have the wish I wish tonight.

Anonymous

Hush Little Baby

Hush little baby, don't say a word,
Papa's gonna buy you a mockingbird.

And if that mockingbird won't sing,
Papa's gonna buy you a diamond ring.

And if that diamond ring turns brass,
Papa's gonna buy you a looking glass.

And if that looking glass gets broke,
Papa's gonna buy you a billy goat.

And if that billy goat won't pull,
Papa's gonna buy you a cart and bull.

And if that cart and bull fall down,
You'll still be the sweetest little baby in town.

Anonymous

Sleep, Baby, Sleep!

Sleep, baby, sleep!
Your father herds his sheep:
Your mother shakes the little tree
From which fall pretty dreams on thee;
Sleep, baby, sleep!

Sleep, baby, sleep!
The heavens are white with sheep:
For they are lambs – those stars so bright:
And the moon's shepherd of the night;
Sleep, baby, sleep!

Sleep, baby, sleep!
And I'll give thee a sheep,
Which, with its golden bell, shall be
A little play-fellow for thee;
Sleep, baby, sleep!

Sleep, baby, sleep!
And bleat not like a sheep,
Or else the shepherd's angry dog
Will come and bite my naughty rogue;
Sleep, baby, sleep!

Sleep, baby, sleep!
Go out and herd the sheep,
Go out, you barking black dog, go,
And waken not my baby so;
Sleep, baby, sleep!

Anonymous

LOVE
and
ADVENTURE

Robin Hood

In Sherwood lived stout Robin Hood,
  An Archer great none greater.
His bow and shafts were sure and good,
  Yet Cupid's were much better.
Robin could shoot at many a Hart and miss,
  Cupid at first could hit a heart of his.
    Hey jolly Robin,
    Hoe jolly Robin,
    Hey jolly Robin Hood,
    Love finds out me
    As well as thee
    To follow me to the green wood.

A noble thief was Robin Hood,
  Wise was he could deceive him,
Yet Marian in his bravest mood
  Could of his heart bereave him,
No greater thief lies hidden under skies
  Than beauty closely lodged in women's eyes.
    Hey jolly Robin,
    Hoe jolly Robin,
    Hey jolly Robin Hood,
    Love finds out me
    As well as thee
    To follow me to the green wood.

Robert Jones

A Red, Red Rose

My love is like a red, red rose,
That's newly sprung in June:
My love is like the melody
That's sweetly played in tune.

As fair art thou, my bonnie lass,
So deep in love am I:
And I will love thee still, my dear,
Till a' the seas gang dry.

Till a' the seas gang dry, my dear,
And the rocks melt wi' the sun:
And I will love thee still, my dear,
While the sands o' life shall run.

And fare thee weel, my only love,
And fare thee weel a while!
And I will come again, my love,
Thou' it were ten thousand mile.

Robert Burns

A Birthday

My heart is like a singing bird
  Whose nest is in a watered shoot;
My heart is like an apple-tree
  Whose boughs are bent with thickset fruit;
My heart is like a rainbow shell
  That paddles in a halcyon sea;
My heart is gladder than all these,
  Because my love is come to me.

Raise me a dais of silk and down;
  Hang it with vair and purple dyes;
Carve it in doves and pomegranates,
  And peacocks with a hundred eyes;
Work it in gold and silver grapes,
  In leaves and silver fleurs-de-lys;
Because the birthday of my life
  Is come, my love is come to me.

Christina Rossetti

Lochinvar

O, young Lochinvar is come out of the west,
Through all the wide Border his steed was the best;
And save his good broadsword he weapons had none,
He rode all unarmed, and he rode all alone.
So faithful in love, and so dauntless in war,
There never was knight like the young Lochinvar.

He stayed not for brake, and he stopped not for stone,
He swam the Eske river where ford there was none;
But ere he alighted at Netherby gate,
The bride had consented, the gallant came late:
For a laggard in love, and a dastard in war,
Was to wed the fair Ellen of brave Lochinvar.

So boldly he entered the Netherby Hall,
Among bride's-men, and kinsmen, and brothers, and all:
Then spoke the bride's father, his hand on his sword,
(For the poor craven bridegroom said never a word)
"O, come ye in peace here, or come ye in war,
Or to dance at our bridal, young Lord Lochinvar?"

"I long wooed your daughter, my suit you denied; –
Love swells like the Solway, but ebbs like its tide –
And now am I come, with this lost love of mine,
To lead but one measure, drink one cup of wine.
There are maidens in Scotland more lovely by far,
That would gladly be bride to the young Lochinvar."

The bride kissed the goblet: the knight took it up,
He quaffed off the wine, and he threw down the cup,
She looked down to blush, and she looked up to sigh,
With a smile on her lips, and a tear in her eye.
He took her soft hand, ere her mother could bar, –
"Now tread we a measure!" said the young Lochinvar.

So stately his form, and so lovely her face,
That never a hall such a galliard did grace;
While her mother did fret, and her father did fume,
And the bridegroom stood dangling his bonnet and plume;
And the bride-maidens whispered "'Twere better by far,
To have matched our fair cousin with young Lochinvar."

One touch to her hand, and one word in her ear,
When they reached the hall-door, and the charger stood near;
So light to the croupe the fair lady he swung,
So light to the saddle before her he sprung!
"She is won! we are gone, over bank, bush, and scaur;
They'll have fleet steeds that follow," quoth young Lochinvar.

There was mounting 'mong Graemes of the Netherby clan;
Forsters, Fenwicks, and Musgraves, they rode and they ran:
There was racing and chasing on Cannobie Lee,
But the lost bride of Netherby ne'er did they see.
So daring in love, and so dauntless in war,
Have ye e'er heard of gallant like young Lochinvar?

Sir Walter Scott

A Newly Courtley Sonnet of the Lady Greensleeves

Alas my love, ye do me wrong,
To cast me off discourteously;
And I have loved you so long,
Delighting in your company.
Greensleeves was all my joy,
Greensleeves was my delight;
Greensleeves was my heart of gold,
And who but my Lady Greensleeves.

I have been ready at your hand,
To grant whatever you would crave;
I have both waged life and land,
Your love and goodwill for to have.

I bought three kerchers to thy head,
That were wrought fine and gallantly;
I kept thee both board and bed,
Which cost my purse well favouredly.

I bought thee petticoats of the best,
The cloth so fine as might be;
I gave thee jewels for thy chest,
And all this cost I spent on thee.

Thy purse and eke thy gay gild knives,
Thy pincase gallant to the eye;
No better wore the burgess wives,
And yet thou wouldst not love me.

Thy gown was of the grassy green,
Thy sleeves of satin hanging by,
Which made thee be our harvest queen,
And yet thou wouldst not love me.

My gayest gelding I thee gave,
To ride wherever liked thee;
No lady ever was so brave,
And yet thou wouldst not love me.

My men were clothed all in green,
And they did ever wait on thee;
All this was gallant to be seen,
And yet thou wouldst not love me.

For every morning when thou rose,
I sent thee dainties orderly,
To cheer thy stomach from all woes,
And yet thou wouldst not love me.

Well, I will pray to God on high,
That thou my constancy mayst see,
And that yet once before I die,
Thou wilt vouchsafe to love me.

Greensleeves, now farewell! adieu!
God I pray to prosper thee;
For I am still thy lover true,
Come once again and love me.
Greensleeves was all my joy, etc.

Anonymous, but some say
King Henry VIII

The Night Has a Thousand Eyes

The night has a thousand eyes,
And the day but one;
Yet the light of the bright world dies
With the dying sun.

The mind has a thousand eyes,
And the heart but one;
Yet the light of a whole life dies
When love is done.

Francis William Bourdillon

SONGS
and
BALLADS

Thomas the Rhymer

True Thomas lay o'er yond grassy bank,
  And he beheld a ladie gay,
A ladie that was brisk and bold,
   Come riding o'er the fernie brae.

Her skirt was of the grass-green silk,
  Her mantle of the velvet fine,
At ilka tett of her horse's mane
  Hung fifty silver bells and nine.

True Thomas he took off his hat,
  And bowed him low down till his knee:
All hail, thou mighty Queen of Heaven!
  For your peer on earth I never did see.

O no, O no, True Thomas, she says,
  That name does not belong to me;
I am but the queen of fair Elfland,
  And I'm come here for to visit thee.

But ye maun go wi' me now, Thomas,
  True Thomas, ye maun go wi' me,
For ye maun serve me seven years,
  Thro weel or wae as may chance to be.

She turned about her milk-white steed,
  And took True Thomas up behind,
And aye whene'er her bridle rang,
  The steed flew swifter than the wind.

O they rade on, and further on,
  Until they came to a garden green:
Light down, light down, ye ladie free,
  Some of that fruit let me pull to thee.

O no, O no, True Thomas, she says,
  That fruit maun not be touched by thee,
For a' the plagues that are in hell
  Light on the fruit of this countrie.

But I have a loaf here in my lap,
  Likewise a bottle of claret wine,
And now 'ere we go farther on,
  We'll rest a while, and ye may dine.

When he had eaten and drunk his fill,
    Lay down your head upon my knee,
The lady sayd, 'ere we climb yon hill,
    And I will show you fairlies three.

O see not ye yon narrow road,
    So thick beset wi' thorns and briers?
That is the path of righteousness,
    Tho after it but few enquires.

And see not ye that braid braid road,
    That lies across yon lillie leven?
That is the path of wickedness,
    Tho some call it the road to heaven.

And see not ye that bonny road,
    Which winds about the fernie brae?
That is the road to fair Elfland,
    Where you and I this night maun gae.

But Thomas, ye maun hold your tongue,
  Whatever you may hear or see,
For gin ae word you should chance to speak,
  You will ne'er get back to your ain countrie.

For forty days and forty nights
  He wade thro red blude to the knee,
And he saw either sun nor moon,
  But heard the roaring of the sea.

He has gooten a coat of the even cloth,
  And a pair of shoes of velvet green,
And till seven years were past and gone
  True Thomas on earth was never seen.

Anonymous

Bonny Barbara Allan

It was in and about the Martinmas time,
When the green leaves were a-falling,
That Sir John Graeme, in the West Country,
Fell in love with Barbara Allan.

He sent his man down through the town,
To the place where she was dwelling,
O haste, and come to my master dear,
Gin ye be Barbara Allan.

O hooly, hooly rose she up,
To the place where he was lying,
And when she drew the curtain by,
Young man, I think you're dying.

O it's I'm sick, and very, very sick,
And 'tis a' for Barbara Allan,
O the better for me ye's never be,
Tho your heart's blood were a-spilling.

O dinna ye mind, young man, said she,
When ye was in the tavern a-drinking,
That ye made the healths gae round and round,
And slighted Barbara Allan?

He turned his face unto the wall,
And death was with him dealing;
Adieu, adieu, my dear friends all,
And be kind to Barbara Allan.

And slowly, slowly raise she up,
And slowly, slowly left him;
And sighing said, she could not stay,
Since death of life had reft him.

She had not gane a mile but twa,
When she heard the dead-bell ringing,
And every jow that the dead-bell gied,
It cry'd, Woe to Barbara Allan!

O mother, mother, make my bed,
O make it saft and narrow,
Since my love died for me today,
I'll die for him tomorrow.

Anonymous

The Great Silkie of Sule Skerrie

An earthly nourris sits and sings,
    And aye she sings, Ba, lily wean!
Little ken I my bairn's father,
    Far less the land that he staps in.

Then ane arose at her bed-fit,
    An' a grumly guest I'm sure was he:
Here am I, thy bairn's father,
    Although that I be not comelie.

I am a man, upon the land,
    An' I am a silkie in the sea,
And when I'm far and far frae land,
    My dwelling is in Sule Skerry.

It was na weel, quo' the maiden fair,
  It was na weel, indeed, quo' she,
That the Great Silkie of Sule Skerry
  Should hae come and aught a bairn to me.

Now he has ta'en a purse of goud,
  And he has put it upo' her knee,
Sayin', Gie to me my little young son,
  An' tak thee up thy nourrice-fee.

An' it sall pass on a summer's day,
  When the sun shines het on evera stane,
That I will tak my little young son,
  An' teach him for to swim the faem.

An' thu sall marry a proud gunner,
  An' a proud gunner I'm sure he'll be,
An' the very first shot that ere he shoots,
  He'll shoot baith my young son and me.

Anonymous

The Yarn of the *Nancy Bell*

'Twas on the shores that round our coast
From Deal to Ramsgate span,
That I found alone on a piece of stone
An elderly naval man.

His hair was weedy, his beard was long,
And weedy and long was he,
And I heard this wight on the shore recite,
In a singular minor key:

"Oh, I am a cook and a captain bold,
And the mate of the *Nancy* brig,
And a bo'sun tight, and a midshipmite,
And the crew of the captain's gig."

And he shook his fists and he tore his hair,
Till I really felt afraid,
For I couldn't help thinking the man had been drinking,
And so I simply said:

"O, elderly man, it's little I know
Of the duties of men of the sea,
But I'll eat my hand if I understand
How you can possibly be

"At once a cook, and a captain bold,
And the mate of the *Nancy* brig,
And a bo'sun tight, and a midshipmite,
And the crew of the captain's gig."

Then he gave a hitch to his trousers, which
Is a trick all seamen larn,
And having got rid of a thumping quid,
He spun this painful yarn:

"'Twas in the good ship *Nancy Bell*
That we sailed to the Indian sea
And there on a reef we come to grief,
Which has often occurred to me.

"And pretty nigh all o' the crew was drowned
(There was seventy-seven o' soul),
And only ten of the *Nancy*'s men
Said 'Here!' to the muster-roll.

"There was me and the cook and the captain bold,
And the mate of the *Nancy* brig
And the bo'sun tight, and a midshipmite,
And the crew of the captain's gig.

"For a month we'd neither wittles nor drink,
Till a-hungry we did feel,
So we drawed a lot, and accordin' shot
The captain for our meal.

"The next lot fell to the *Nancy*'s mate,
And a delicate dish he made;
Then our appetite with the midshipmite
We seven survivors stayed.

"And then we murdered the bo'sun tight,
And he much resembled pig;
Then we wittled free, did the cook and me,
On the crew of the captain's gig.

"Then only the cook and me was left,
And the delicate question, 'Which
Of us two goes to the kettle?' arose,
And we argued it out as sich.

"For I loved that cook as a brother, I did,
And the cook he worshipped me;
But we'd both be blowed if we'd either be stowed
In the other chap's hold, you see.

"'I'll be eat if you dines off me,' says Tom,
'Yes, that,' says I, 'you'll be,' –
'I'm boiled if I die, my friend,' quoth I,
And 'Exactly so,' quoth he.

"Says he, 'Dear James, to murder me
Were a foolish thing to do,
For don't you see that you can't cook me,
While I can – and will – cook *you*!'

"So he boils the water, and takes the salt
And the pepper in portions true
(Which he never forgot) and some chopped shallot,
And some sage and parsley too.

"'Come here,' says he, with a proper pride,
  Which his smiling features tell,
''Twill soothing be if I let you see,
  How extremely nice you'll smell.'

"And he stirred it round and round and round,
  And he sniffed at the foaming froth;
When I ups with his heels, and smothers his squeals
  In the scum of the boiling broth.

"And I eat that cook in a week or less,
  And – as I eating be
The last of his chops, why, I almost drops,
  For a wessel in sight I see!

"And I never grin, and I never smile,
  And I never lark nor play,
But I sit and croak, and a single joke
  I have – which is to say:

"Oh, I am a cook and a captain bold,
  And the mate of the *Nancy* brig,
And a bo'sun tight, and a midshipmite,
  And the crew of the captain's gig!"

Sir W. S. Gilbert

Boys
and
Girls

What Am I After All

What am I after all but a child, pleas'd with the sound
     of my own name? repeating it over and over;
I stand apart to hear – it never tires me.

To you your name also;
Did you think there was nothing but two or three
     pronunciations in the sound of your name?

Walt Whitman

Jemima

There was a little girl, and she wore a little curl
      Right down the middle of her forehead,
When she was good, she was very, very, good,
      But when she was bad, she was horrid!

One day she went upstairs, while her parents, unawares,
      In the kitchen down below were occupied with meals,
And she stood upon her head, on her little truckle bed,
      And she then began hurraying with her heels.

Her mother heard the noise, and thought it was the boys
      A-playing at a combat in the attic,
But when she climbed the stair and saw Jemima there,
      She took and she did whip her most emphatic.

Anonymous

There Was a Naughty Boy

There was a naughty Boy,
    A naughty Boy was he,
He would not stop at home,
He could not quiet be –
    He took
    In his Knapsack
    A Book
    Full of vowels
    And a shirt
    With some towels –
    A slight cap
    For night cap –
    A hair brush
    Comb ditto
    New Stockings
    For old ones
    Would split O!
    This Knapsack
    Tight at's back
    He rivetted close
And follow'd his Nose
    To the North
    To the North
And follow'd his nose
    To the North.

There was a naughty Boy
    And a naughty Boy was he,
He ran way to Scotland
    The people for to see –
        There he found
        That the ground
        Was as hard
        That a yard
        Was as long,
        That a song
        Was as merry,
        That a cherry
        Was as red –
        That lead
        Was as weighty
        That forescore
        Was as eighty
        That a door
        Was as wooden
        As in England –
        So he stood in
        His shoes
        And he wonder'd
        He stood in his
        Shoes and he wonder'd.

John Keats

The False Knight and the Wee Boy

"O whare are ye gaun?"
      Quo' the fause knicht upon the road:
"I'm gaun to the scule,"
      Quo' the wee boy, and still he stude.

"What is that upon your back?"
      Quo' the fause knicht upon the road:
"Atweel it is my bukes,"
      Quo' the wee boy, and still he stude.

"Wha's aucht thae sheep?"
      Quo' the fause knicht upon the road:
"They are mine and my mither's,"
      Quo' the wee boy, and still he stude.

"How mony o' them are mine?"
        Quo' the fause knicht upon the road:
"A' they that hae blue tails,"
        Quo' the wee boy, and still he stude.

"I wiss ye were on yon tree?"
        Quo' the fause knicht upon the road:
"And for you to fa' down,"
        Quo' the wee boy, and still he stude.

"I wiss ye were in yon sie,"
        Quo' the fause knicht upon the road:
"And a gude bottom under me,"
        Quo' the wee boy, and still he stude.

"And the bottom for to break?"
        Quo' the fause knicht upon the road:
"And ye to be drowned,"
        Quo' the wee boy, and still he stude.

                    Anonymous

Children

Come to me, O ye children!
For I hear you at your play,
And the questions that perplexed me
Have vanished quite away.

Ye open the eastern windows,
That look towards the sun,
Where thoughts are singing swallows
And the brooks of morning run.

In your hearts are the birds and the sunshine,
In your thoughts the brooklet's flow,
But in mine is the wind of Autumn
And the first fall of the snow.

Ah! what would the world be to us
If the children were no more?
We should dread the desert behind us
Worse than the dark before.

What the leaves are to the forest,
  With light and air for food,
Ere their sweet and tender juices
Have been hardened into wood, –

That to the world are children;
  Through them it feels the glow
Of a brighter and sunnier climate
  Than reaches the trunks below.

Come to me, O ye children!
  And whisper in my ear
What the birds and the winds are singing
  In your sunny atmosphere.

For what are all our contrivings,
  And the wisdom of our books,
When compared with your caresses,
  And the gladness of your looks?

Ye are better than all the ballads
  That ever were sung or said;
  For ye are living poems,
  And all the rest are dead.

Henry Wadsworth Longfellow

When That I Was and a Little Tiny Boy

When that I was and a little tiny boy,
    With hey, ho, the wind and the rain;
A foolish thing was but a toy,
    For the rain it raineth every day.

But when I came to man's estate,
    With hey, ho, the wind and the rain;
'Gainst knaves and thieves men shut their gate,
    For the rain it raineth every day.

But when I came, alas! to wive,
    With hey, ho, the wind and the rain;
By swaggering could I never thrive,
    For the rain it raineth every day.

But when I came unto my beds,
     With hey, ho, the wind and the rain;
With toss-pots still had drunken heads,
     For the rain it raineth every day.

A great while ago the world began,
     With hey, ho, the wind and the rain;
But that's all one, our play is done,
     And we'll strive to please you every day.

William Shakespeare

MAGIC
and
MYSTERY

Waltzing Matilda

Once a jolly swagman camped by a billabong,
Under the shade of a coolabah tree;
And he sang as he watched and waited till his billy boiled,
"You'll come a-waltzing Matilda with me!"

*"Waltzing Matilda, Waltzing Matilda,
You'll come a-waltzing Matilda with me,"
And he sang as he watched and waited till his billy boiled,
"You'll come a-waltzing Matilda with me."*

Down came a jumbuck to drink at the billabong,
Up jumped the swagman and grabbed him with glee;
And he sang as he shoved the jumbuck in his tucker-bag,
"You'll come a-waltzing Matilda with me."

*"Waltzing Matilda, Waltzing Matilda,
You'll come a-waltzing Matilda with me,"
And he sang as he shoved that jumbuck in his tucker-bag,
"You'll come a-waltzing Matilda with me."*

Up rode the squatter mounted on his thoroughbred;
Down came troopers – one, two and three.
"Who's that jolly jumbuck you've got in your tucker-bag?
You'll come a-waltzing Matilda with me."

*"Waltzing Matilda, Waltzing Matilda,
You'll come a-waltzing Matilda with me,
Who's that jolly jumbuck you've got in your tucker-bag?
You'll come a-waltzing Matilda with me."*

Up jumped the swagman, sprang into the billabong,
"You'll never catch me alive," said he.
And his ghost may be heard as you pass by that billabong,
"Who'll come a-waltzing Matilda with me?"

*"Waltzing Matilda, Waltzing Matilda,
You'll come a-waltzing Matilda with me,"
And his ghost may be heard as you pass by that billabong,
"Who'll come a-waltzing Matilda with me?"*

A. B. Paterson

The Ghost's Song

Wae's me! wae's me!
The acorn's not yet
Fallen from the tree
That's to grow the wood,
That's to make the cradle,
That's to rock the bairn,
That's to grow a man,
That's to lay me.

Anonymous

John Barleycorn

There was three Kings into the east,
    Three Kings both great and high,
And they hae sworn a solemn oath
    John Barleycorn should die.

They took a plough and plough'd him down,
    Put clods upon his head,
And they hae sworn a solemn oath
    John Barleycorn was dead.

But the cheerfu' Spring came kindly on,
    And show'rs began to fall;
John Barleycorn got up again,
    And sore surprised them all.

The sultry suns of Summer came,
    And he grew thick and strong,
His head weel arm'd wi' pointed spears,
    That no one should him wrong.

The sober Autumn enter'd mild,
    When he grew wan and pale;
His bending joints and drooping head
    Show'd he began to fail.

His colour sicken'd more and more,
    He faded into age;
And then his enemies began
    To shew their deadly rage.

They've ta'en a weapon, long and sharp,
    And cut him by the knee;
Then tied him fast upon a cart,
    Like a rogue for forgerie.

They laid him down upon his back,
    And cudgell'd him full sore;
They hung him up before the storm,
    And turn'd him o'er and o'er.

They filled up a darksome pit
    With water to the brim,
They heaved in John Barleycorn,
    There let him sink or swim.

They laid him out upon the floor,
    To work him further woe,
And still, as signs of life appear'd,
    They toss'd him to and fro.

They wasted, o'er a scorching flame,
    The marrow of his bones;
But a miller us'd him worst of all,
    For he crush'd him between two stones.

And they hae ta'en his very heart's blood,
    And drank it round and round;
And still the more and more they drank,
    Their joy did more abound.

John Barleycorn was a hero bold,
    Of noble enterprise,
For if you do but taste his blood,
    'Twill make your courage rise.

'Twill make a man forget his woe;
    'Twill heighten all his joy:
'Twill make the widow's heart to sing,
    Tho' the tear were in her eye.

Then let us toast John Barleycorn,
    Each man a glass in hand;
And may his great posterity
    Ne'er fail in old Scotland!

Robert Burns

A Strange Visitor

A wife, was sitting at her reel ae night;
And aye she sat, and aye she reeled, and aye she wished for company.

In came a pair o' braid braid soles, and sat down at the fireside;
And aye she sat, and aye she reeled, and aye she wished for company.

In came a pair o' sma' sma' legs, and sat down on the braid braid soles;
And aye she sat, and aye she reeled, and aye she wished for company.

In came a pair o' muckle muckle knees, and sat down on the sma' sma' legs;
And aye she sat, and aye she reeled, and aye she wished for company.

In came a pair o' sma' sma' thees, and sat down on the muckle muckle knees;
And aye she sat, and aye she reeled, and aye she wished for company.

In came a pair o' muckle muckle hips, and sat down on the sma' sma' thees;
And aye she sat, and aye she reeled, and aye she wished for company.

In came a sma' sma' waist, and sat down on the muckle muckle hips;
And aye she sat, and aye she reeled, and aye she wished for company.

In came a pair o' braid braid shouthers, and sat down on the sma' sma' waist;
And aye she sat, and aye she reeled, and aye she wished for company.

In came a pair o' sma' sma' arms, and sat down on the braid braid shouthers;
And aye she sat, and aye she reeled, and aye she wished for company.

In came a pair o' muckle muckle hands, and sat down on the sma' sma' arms;
And aye she sat, and aye she reeled, and aye she wished for company.

In came a sma' sma' neck, and sat down on the braid braid shouthers;
And aye she sat, and aye she reeled, and aye she wished for company.

In came a great big head, and sat down on the sma' sma' neck;
And aye she sat, and aye she reeled, and aye she wished for company.

"What way hae ye sic braid braid feet?" quo' the wife.
"Muckle ganging, muckle ganging."
"What way hae ye sic sma' sma' legs?"
"*Aih-h-h!* – late – and *wee-e-e* moul."
"What way hae ye sic muckle muckle knees?"
"Muckle praying, muckle praying."
"What way hae ye sic sma' sma' thees?"
"*Aih-h-h!* – late – and *wee-e-e* moul."
"What way hae ye sic big big hips?
"Muckle sitting, muckle sitting"
"What way hae ye sic a sma' sma' waist?"
"*Aih-h-h!* – late – and *wee-e-e* moul."
"What way hae ye sic braid braid shouthers?"
"Wi' carrying broom, wi' carrying broom."
"What way hae ye sic sma' sma' arms?
"*Aih-h-h!* – late – and *wee-e-e* moul."
"What way hae ye sic muckle muckle hands?"
"Threshing wi' an iron flail, threshing wi' an iron flail."
"What way hae ye sic a sma' sma' neck?
"*Aih-h-h!* – late – and *wee-e-e* moul."
"What way hae ye sic a muckle muckle head?"
"Muckle wit, muckle wit."
"What do you come for?"
"For YOU!"

Anonymous

The Oxen

Christmas Eve, and twelve of the clock.
    "Now they are all on their knees,"
An elder said as we sat in a flock
    By the embers in hearthside ease.

We pictured the meek mild creatures where
    They dwelt in their strawy pen,
Nor did it occur to one of us there
    To doubt they were kneeling then.

So fair a fancy few would weave
    In these years! Yet, I feel,
If someone said on Christmas Eve,
    "Come; see the oxen kneel,

"In the lonely barton by yonder coomb
    Our childhood used to know,"
I should go with him in the gloom,
    Hoping it might be so.

Thomas Hardy

SIGHTS
and
SOUNDS

Upon Westminster Bridge

Earth has not anything to show more fair:
Dull would he be of soul who could pass by
A sight so touching in its majesty:
This City now doth, like a garment, wear
The beauty of the morning; silent, bare,
Ships, towers, domes, theatres, and temples lie
Open unto the fields, and to the sky;
All bright and glittering in the smokeless air.
Never did sun more beautifully steep
In his first splendour valley, rock, or hill;
Ne'er saw I, never felt, a calm so deep!
The river glideth at his own sweet will:
Dear God! the very houses seem asleep;
And all that mighty heart is lying still!

William Wordsworth

On First Looking into Chapman's Homer

Much have I travell'd in the realms of gold,
 And many goodly states and kingdoms seen;
 Round many western islands have I been
Which bards in fealty to Apollo hold.
Oft of one wide expanse had I been told
 That deep-brow'd Homer ruled as his demesne;
 Yet did I never breathe its pure serene
Till I heard Chapman speak out loud and bold:
Then felt I like some watcher of the skies
 When a new planet swims into his ken;
Or like stout Cortez, when with eagle eyes
 He star'd at the Pacific – and all his men
Look'd at each other with a wild surmise –
 Silent, upon a peak in Darien.

John Keats

Symphony in Yellow

An omnibus across the bridge
Crawls like a yellow butterfly,
And, here and there, a passer-by
Shows like a little restless midge.

Big barges full of yellow hay
Are moored against the shadowy wharf,
And, like a yellow silken scarf,
The thick fog hangs along the quay.

The yellow leaves begin to fade
And flutter from the Temple elms,
And at my feet the pale green Thames
Lies like a rod of rippled jade.

Oscar Wilde

A Thing of Beauty

A thing of beauty is a joy for ever:
Its loveliness increases; it will never
Pass into nothingness; but still will keep
A bower quiet for us, and a sleep
Full of sweet dreams, and health, and quiet breathing.
Therefore, on every morrow, are we wreathing
A flowery band to bind us to the earth,
Spite of despondence, of the inhuman death
Of noble natures, of the gloomy days,
Of all the unhealthy and o'er-darkn'd ways
Made for our searching: yes, in spite of all,
Some shape of beauty moves away the pall
From our dark spirits.

John Keats

From The Garden

What wondrous life is this I lead!
Ripe apples drop about my head;
The luscious clusters of the vine
Upon my mouth do crush their wine;
The nectarine, and curious peach,
Into my hands themselves do reach;
Stumbling on melons, as I pass,
Ensnared with flowers, I fall on grass.

Meanwhile the mind, from pleasure less,
Withdraws into its happiness:
The mind, that ocean where each kind
Does straight its own resemblance find;
Yet it creates, transcending these,
Far other worlds, and other seas;
Annihilating all that's made
To a green thought in a green shade.

Andrew Marvell

MUSIC
and
DANCING

Song's Eternity

What is song's eternity?
      Come and see.
Can it noise and bustle be?
      Come and see.
Praises sung or praises said
      Can it be?
Wait awhile and these are dead –
      Sigh, sigh;
Be they high or lowly bred
      They die.

What is song's eternity?
      Come and see.
Melodies of earth and sky,
      Here they be.
Song once sung to Adam's ears
      Can it be?
Ballads of six thousand years
      Thrive, thrive;
Songs awaken with the spheres
      Alive.

Mighty songs that miss decay,
      What are they?
Crowds and cities pass away
      Like a day.
Books are out and books are read;
      What are they?
Years will lay them with the dead –
      Sigh, sigh;
Trifles unto nothing wed,
      They die.

Dreamers, mark the honey bee;
      Mark the tree
Where the blue cap *"tootle tee"*
      Sings a glee
Sung to Adam and to Eve –
      Here they be.
When floods covered every bough,
      Noah's ark
Heard that ballad singing now;
      Hark, hark,

"Tootle tootle tootle tee" –
Can it be
Pride and fame must shadows be?
Come and see –
Every season own her own;
Bird and bee
Sing creation's music on;
Nature's glee
Is in every mood and tone
Eternity.

John Clare

The Power of Music

Orpheus with his lute made trees,
    And the mountain-tops that freeze,
Bow themselves when he did sing.
    To his music plants and flowers
Ever sprung: as sun and showers
    There had made a lasting spring.

Everything that heard him play,
    Even the billows of the sea,
Hung their heads, and then lay by.
    In sweet music is such art,
Killing care and grief of heart
    Fall asleep, or, hearing, die.

John Fletcher

Piano

Softly, in the dusk, a woman is singing to me;
Taking me back down the vista of years, till I see
A child sitting under the piano, in the boom of the tingling strings
And pressing the small, poised feet of a mother who smiles as she sings.

In spite of myself, the insidious mastery of song
Betrays me back, till the heart of me weeps to belong
To the old Sunday evenings at home, with winter outside
And hymns in the cosy parlour, the tinkling piano our guide.

So now it is vain for the singer to burst into clamour
With the great black piano appassionato. The glamour
Of childish days is upon me, my manhood is cast
Down in the flood of remembrance, I weep like a child for the past.

D. H. Lawrence

I Am of Ireland

I am of Ireland,
And of the holy land
Of Ireland.

Good sir, pray I thee,
For of saint charity,
Come and dance with me
In Ireland.

Anonymous

To Emilia V–

Music, when soft voices die,
Vibrates in the memory –
Odours, when sweet violets sicken,
Live within the sense they quicken.

Rose leaves, when the rose is dead,
Are heaped for the beloved's bed –
And so thy thoughts, when thou are gone,
Love itself shall slumber on ...

Percy Bysshe Shelley

SADNESS
and
HAPPINESS

So, We'll Go No More A-Roving

So, we'll go no more a-roving
    So late into the night,
Though the heart be still as loving,
    And the moon be still as bright.

For the sword outwears its sheath,
    And the soul wears out the breast,
And the heart must pause to breathe,
    And love itself have rest.

Though the night was made for loving,
    And the day returns too soon,
Yet we'll go no more a-roving
    By the light of the moon.

George Gordon, Lord Byron

Spring and Fall

to a young child

Margaret, are you grieving
Over Goldengrove unleaving?
Leaves, like the things of man, you
With your fresh thoughts care for, can you?
Ah! as the heart grows older
It will come to such sights colder
By and by, nor spare a sigh
Though worlds of wanwood leafmeal lie,
And yet you *will* weep and know why.
Now no matter, child, the name:
Sorrow's springs are the same.
Nor mouth had, no nor mind, expressed
What heart heard of, ghost guessed:
It is the blight man was born for,
It is Margaret you mourn for.

Gerard Manley Hopkins

Canadian Boat Song

Listen to me, as when ye heard our father
Sing long ago the song of other shores –
Listen to me, and then in chorus gather
All your deep voices as ye pull the oars:
    Fair these broad meads – these hoary woods are grand;
    But we are exiles from our fathers' land.

From the lone shieling of the misty island
Mountains divide us, and the waste of seas,
Yet still the blood is strong, the heart is Highland,
And we in dreams behold the Hebrides.

We ne'er shall tread the fancy-haunted valley,
Where 'tween the dark hills creeps the small clear stream,
In arms around the patriarch banner rally,
Nor see the moon on royal tombstones gleam.

When the bold kindred in the time long-vanished,
Conquered the soil and fortified the keep –
No seer foretold the children would be banished,
That a degenerate lord might boast his sheep.

Come foreigner rage – let Discord burst in slaughter!
O then for clansmen true, and stern claymore,
The hearts that would have given their blood like water,
Beat heavily beyond the Atlantic roar.
    Fair these broad meads – these hoary woods are grand;
    But we are exiles from our fathers' land.

Anonymous

In the Highlands

In the highlands, in the country places,
Where the old plain men have rosy faces,
And the young fair maidens
Quiet eyes;
Where essential silence cheers and blesses,
And for ever in the hill-recesses
Her more lovely music
Broods and dies.

O to mount again where erst I haunted;
Where the old red hills are bird-enchanted,
And the low green meadows
Bright with sward;
And when even dies, the million-tinted,
And the night has come, and planets glinted,
Lo, the valley hollow
Lamp-bestarred!

O to dream, O to awake and wander
There, and with delight to take and render,
Through the trance of silence,
Quiet breath;
Lo! for there, among the flowers and grasses,
Only the mightier movement sounds and passes;
Only winds and rivers,
Life and death.

Robert Louis Stevenson

When in Disgrace With Fortune

When, in disgrace with fortune and men's eyes
I all alone beweep my outcast state,
And trouble deaf heaven with my bootless cries,
And look upon myself and curse my fate,
Wishing me like to one more rich in hope,
Featured like him, like him with friends possessed,
Desiring this man's art and that man's scope,
With what I most enjoy contented least;
Yet in these thoughts myself almost despising,
Haply I think on thee, and then my state,
(Like to the lark at break of day arising
From sullen earth) sings hymns at heaven's gate;
    For thy sweet love remembered such wealth brings,
    That then I scorn to change my state with kings.

William Shakespeare

Piping Down the Valleys Wild

Piping down the valleys wild,
Piping songs of pleasant glee,
On a cloud I saw a child,
And he laughing said to me:

"Pipe a song about a Lamb!"
So I piped with merry cheer.
"Piper, pipe that song again."
So I piped: he wept to hear.

"Drop thy pipe, thy happy pipe;
Sing thy songs of happy cheer."
So I sung the same again,
While he wept with joy to hear.

"Piper, sit thee down and write
In a book, that all may read."
So he vanish'd from my sight,
And I pluck'd a hollow reed,

And I made a rural pen,
And I stain'd the water clear,
And I wrote my happy songs
Every child may joy to hear.

William Blake

A Lark's Nest

Now's the time for mirth and play,
Saturday's an holiday;
Praise to heav'n unceasing yield,
I've found a lark's nest in the field.

A lark's nest, then your play-mate begs
You'd spare herself and speckled eggs;
Soon she shall ascend and sing
Your praise to th'eternal King.

Christopher Smart

From The Song of Solomon

My beloved spake, and said unto me, Rise up, my love, my fair one, and
    come away.
For, lo, the winter is past, the rain is over and gone;
The flowers appear on the earth, the time of the singing of birds is come,
    and the voice of the turtle is heard in our land.
The fig tree putteth forth her green figs, and the vines with the tender
grape give a good smell.
Arise, my love, my fair one, and come away.

King James Bible

The Swing

How do you like to go up in a swing,
Up in the air so blue?
Oh, I do think it the pleasantest thing
Ever a child can do!

Up in the air and over the wall,
Till I can see so wide,
River and trees and cattle and all
Over the countryside –

Till I look down on the garden green,
Down on the roof so brown –
Up in the air I go flying again,
Up in the air and down!

Robert Louis Stevenson

Requiem

Under the wide and starry sky,
Dig the grave and let me lie.
Glad did I live and gladly die,
And I laid me down with a will.

This be the verse you grave for me:
Here he lies where he longed to be;
Home is the sailor, home from the sea,
And the hunter home from the hill.

Robert Louis Stevenson

ABOUT the POETS

WILLIAM ALLINGHAM
1824–89
Pages 57, 92. This Irish poet wrote
many volumes of poetry, including
some based on traditional Irish myths
and legends.

WILLIAM BLAKE
1757–1827
Pages 18, 26, 38, 48, 177. Born in
London, Blake was a painter and
engraver as well as a poet.
He illustrated many of his own
poems with vivid engravings.

FRANCIS WILLIAM BOURDILLON
1852–1921
Page 115. Bourdillon was an English
poet. This is his best known work.
The first line is based on a line by
the sixteenth-century poet Lyly.

EMILY BRONTË
1818–48
Page 41. One of the three famous
Brontë sisters, Emily is best known for
her only novel, *Wuthering Heights*,
which she published under the
name of Ellis Bell.

ROBERT BROWNING
1812–89
Page 42, 73. Browning's poems
attracted much attention during his
lifetime, including that of fellow poet
Elizabeth Barrett. They were
married in 1846.

ROBERT BURNS
1759–96
Page 107, 147. This Scottish poet was
very famous during his lifetime for his
poems and songs. He worked on a farm
in his early years and later, when his
writing had brought him wealth,
bought his own farm.

GEORGE GORDON, LORD BYRON
1788–1824
Page 50, 170. A romantic figure,
very popular during his lifetime,
Byron died of fever in Greece,
supporting a Greek uprising.

LEWIS CARROLL
1832–98
Page 14, 17. Lewis Carroll's real name
was Charles Dodgson. He became
famous for his children's books, *Alice's
Adventures in Wonderland* and *Through
the Looking Glass*.

JOHN CLARE
1794–1864
Page 162. Although he had little
education, John Clare wrote movingly
about the countryside and his feelings
of loss and sadness. His life was
difficult and often unhappy, but his
poems still move us today.

ARTHUR HUGH CLOUGH
1819–61
Page 77. Clough's father emigrated to the USA. His son returned to England to live and work, but had many American friends.

SAMUEL TAYLOR COLERIDGE
1772–1834
Page 54. A poet and philosopher, Coleridge was a great friend of the poet William Wordsworth.

EMILY DICKINSON
1830–36
Page 68. This American poet lived a secluded life in Massachusetts, writing over a thousand poems. Their original forms and use of language have influenced many modern poets.

EUGENE FIELD
1850–95
Page 99. This American journalist is now famous for his poems for children.

JOHN FLETCHER
1579–1625
Page 165. Known mainly as a playwright, Fletcher was writing in London at the same time as Shakespeare and may have worked with him on some plays.

SIR W. S. GILBERT
1836–1911
Page 126. Gilbert is known for his writing the words in the famous musical partnership with Sir Arthur Sullivan.

THOMAS HARDY
1840–1928
Page 154. This poet and novelist was born in the south-west of England, which appears over and over again in his work.

ROBERT HERRICK
1591–1674
Page 89. This English poet wrote chiefly about love, youth and figures from ancient Greece and Rome.

THOMAS HOOD
1799–1845
Page 90. Born in London, this poet and humourist contributed to many popular magazines.

GERARD MANLEY HOPKINS
1844–89
Page 44, 171. As a young man, Hopkins became a Roman Catholic; many of his poems have a religious theme.

ROBERT JONES
lived around 1600
Page 106. Jones wrote songs for several voices, called madrigals, and simpler airs, such as *Robin Hood*, to be sung to the lute, a stringed instrument.

JOHN KEATS
1795–1821
Pages 36, 60, 134, 157, 159. Trained as a doctor, Keats wrote many wonderful poems before dying, still a very young man, in Rome, Italy.

D. H. LAWRENCE
1885–1930
Page 166. The son of a miner, Lawrence wrote several novels set in the mining area of the English Midlands, as well as others reflecting his many travels abroad.

EDWARD LEAR
1812–88
Page 12. An artist and author, Lear wrote many serious books but is best known for his *Book of Nonsense*, published in 1846.

HENRY WADSWORTH LONGFELLOW
1807–82
Pages 40, 138. As well as short poems, Longfellow enjoyed telling long stores in verse, such as *Hiawatha*.

ANDREW MARVELL
1621–78
Page 160. Marvell spent the early part of his working life as a tutor to wealthy families. Later, he became an energetic politician and a defender of the poet John Milton.

HERMAN MELVILLE
1819–91
Page 21. Born in New York, Melville is perhaps most famous for his sea-faring novel, *Moby Dick*.

A. B. PATERSON
1864–1941
Page 144. The famous Australian poem *Waltzing Matilda* has been attributed to this poet, although some people think it was based on an older ballad.

EDGAR ALLAN POE
1809–49
Page 78. This American poet and story-teller particularly enjoyed mysterious and spine-chilling subjects.

JAMES WHITCOMB RILEY
1849–1916
Page 86. This American poet was born in Indiana. *Little Orphant Annie* is his most famous poem.

CHRISTINA ROSSETTI
1830–94
Pages 16, 32, 33, 67, 81, 98, 108. The poet's Italian father settled in London before her birth. She also has a famous brother, the painter and poet Dante Gabriel Rossetti.

SIR WALTER SCOTT
1771–1832
Pages 20, 109. A poet and a novelist, Scott celebrated all things Scottish in his work.

WILLIAM SHAKESPEARE
1564–1616
Pages 37, 51, 66, 140, 176. Perhaps the greatest playwright in the English language, Shakespeare lived in the time of Elizabeth I.

PERCY BYSSHE SHELLEY
1792–1822
Pages 76, 168. Shelley shocked English society with his beliefs. His later years were spent abroad.

CHRISTOPHER SMART
1722–71
Pages 22, 178. As well as writing poetry, Smart also made translations of the Bible.

ROBERT LOUIS STEVENSON
1850–94
Pages 35, 45, 64, 80, 82, 84, 93, 96, 97, 174. A popular writer of adventure stores, Stevenson is perhaps best known for his *Treasure Island*.

ALFRED, LORD TENNYSON
1809–92
Pages 24, 27, 52, 72. Tennyson's poems and verse-stories enjoyed huge popularity in his lifetime.

WALT WHITMAN
1819–92
Pages 70, 132. Whitman's varied life and experiences in the American Civil War are reflected in his poetry, but he did not find real fame until after his death.

OSCAR WILDE
1854–1900
Page 158. Wilde's life ended sadly in France, but his witty and elegant plays are still widely performed today. They include *Lady Windermere's Fan* and *The Importance of Being Ernest*. He also wrote poetry and several stories for children.

WILLIAM WORDSWORTH
1770–1850
Pages 46, 156. Wordsworth is best known as a poet of nature, expressing his love for the Lake District, England.

Glossary

a' all

ae one

ain own

alighted got down from his horse

ane one

atweel know well

aught a bairn to me had a child with me

aye always

bairn child

baith both

barton barn

beweep cry about

billabong dead-end water-filled channel

billy can

blude blood

bootless fruitless

brae brow of a hill

braid broad

brake thicket

bukes books

burgess well-to-do citizen

charger war-horse

chear cheer

claymore broadsword

comelie handsome

coolabah tree kind of gum tree

coomb valley

croup hindquarters (or a horse)

dauntless bomb

demesne estate

dinna don't

eke also

ere before

erst first

even evening

fa' fall

faem foam

fairlies wonders

fause false

fealty loyalty, trust

fernie ferny

fleet fast

fleurs-de-lys iris-flower pattern appearing in heraldry

ford river crossing

frae from

galliard courtly dance

gane gone

gang go

ganging going

gaun going

gied gave

gild gilded

gin if

goud gold

grave carve

grumly fierce-looking

gude good

hae have

halcyon calm

haply by chance

het hot

hoary ancient

hooly gently

ilka every

jow stroke

jumbuck sheep

keep strongest part of castle

ken know, knowledge

kerchers kerchiefs, head-dresses

knaves rogues

knicht knight

larn learn
lay (a ghost) put a ghost to rest
lillie leven lovely glade
lily wean lovely little one
mantel cloak
maun must
meads meadows
mither mother
mony many
muckle great
na not
ne'er never
nigh nearly
nourrice, nourris nurse
o' of
o'er over
omnibus horsedrawn bus
pall gloomy covering
putteth puts
quaffed drank
quid piece of tobacco being chewed
quo' said
quoth said
rade rode
reft torn
saft soft
sall shall
scaur cliff
scule school
shew show
shieling hut on grazing land
shouthers shoulders
sic such
sich such
sie sea
silkie seal
sma' thin

spake spoke
squatter sheepstation owner
stane stone
staps steps
steeds horses
stude stood
Sule Skerrie Seal Reef
swagman tramp carrying a swag
    or bundle
sward grass
ta'en taken
tett lock of hair of mane
thees thighs
thou you
thu you
tucker-bag food bag
turtle turtle dove
twa two
unceasing without stopping
vair fur
wae woe
waged gambled
waltzing Matilda carrying a swag
wan pale
weel well
wessel vessel, ship
wha's aucht thae? whose are those?
whare? where?
what way? why?
wi' with
wight creature
wiss wish
wittles food
wive marry
wrought made
ye you
yon yonder

Index of Titles and First Lines

A Birthday	108
A Child's Grace	89
A Child's Thought	64
A Lark's Nest	178
A New Courtly Sonnet of the	
Lady Greensleeves	112
A Red, Red, Rose	107
A Strange Visitor	151
A Thing of Beauty	159
A thing of beauty is a joy for ever	159
A wife was sitting at her reel ae night	151
About the Shark, phlegmatical one	21
At seven, when I go to bed	64
Alas, my Love! ye do me wrong	112
An earthly nourris sits and sings	124
An omnibus across the bridge	158
Auguries of Innocence	18
Bed in Summer	97
Blow, Bugle, Blow	52
Boats sail on the rivers	32
Bonny Barbara Allan	122
Break, Break, Break	72
Break, Break, Break	72
Canadian Boat Song	172
Children	138
Children, you are very little	93
Christmas Eve, and twelve of the clock	154
Come to me, O ye children!	138
Daffodils	46
Does the road wind uphill all the way?	81
Earth has nothing to show more fair	156
Eldorado	78
Escape at Bedtime	96

Fall, Leaves, Fall	41
Fall, leaves, fall: die, flowers, away	41
Faster than fairies, faster than witches	84
Foreign Lands	80
For I will consider my cat Jeoffry	22
Four seasons will fill the measure	
of the year	36
From a Railway Carriage	84
From *Rain in Summer*	40
From *The Garden*	160
From *The Song of Solomon*	179
Full Fathom Five	66
Full fathom five they father lies	66
Gaily bedight	78
Glory be to God for dappled things	44
Good and Bad Children	93
He clasps the crag with crooked hands	27
Here a little child I stand	89
How beautiful is the rain!	40
How do you like to go up in a swing	180
How Doth the Little Crocodile	17
How doth the little crocodile	17
How Many Miles to Babylon?	101
How many miles to Babylon?	101
Hurt No Living Thing	16
Hurt no living thing	16
Hush Little Baby	102
Hush little baby, don't say a word	102
I Am of Ireland	167
I am of Ireland	167
I have a little shadow that goes in	
and out with me	45
I met a traveller from an antique land	76
I Remember, I Remember	90
I remember, I remember	90

I Saw a Peacock	63
I saw a peacock with a fiery tail	63
I should like to rise and go	82
I Started Early	68
I started Early – Took my Dog	68
In Sherwood lived stout Robin Hood	106
In the Highlands	174
In the highlands, in the country places	174
In winter I get up at night	97
In Xanadu did Kubla Khan	54
I wandered lonely as a cloud	46
Is the Moon Tired?	98
Is the moon tired? She looks so pale	98
It was in and about the Martinmas time	122
It's Raining, It's Pouring	31
It's raining, it's pouring	31
Jabberwocky	14
Jemima	133
John Barleycorn	147
Kubla Khan	54
La Belle Dame Sans Mercie	60
Listen to me, as when ye heard our father	172
Little Orphant Annie	86
Little Orphant Annie's come to our house to stay	86
Lochinvar	109
Margaret, are you grieving?	171
Meeting at Night	73
Monday's Child	88
Monday's child is fair of face	88
Much have I travell'd in the realms of gold	157
Music, when soft voices die	168
My beloved spake, and said unto me, Rise up, my love, my fair one, and come away	179
My Cat Jeoffry	22
My heart is like a singing bird	108
My love is like a red, red rose	107
My Shadow	45
Now's the time for mirth and play	178
O Captain! My Captain!	70
O Captain! my Captain! our fearful trip is done	70
"O whare are ye gaun?"	136
O, what can ail thee, knight-at-arms	60
O, young Lochinvar is come out of the west	109
On First Looking into Chapman's Homer	157
Once a jolly swagman camped by a billabong	144
Orpheus with his lute made trees	165
Ozymandias	76
Piano	166
Pied Beauty	44
Piping down the valleys wild	177
Piping Down the Valleys Wild	177
Requiem	181
Robin Hood	106
Shall I Compare thee to a Summer's Day?	51
Shall I compare thee to a summer's day?	51
She Walks in Beauty	50
She walks in beauty, like the night	50
Sleep, Baby, Sleep!	103
Sleep, baby, sleep!	103
So, We'll Go No More A-Roving	170
So, we'll go no more a-roving	170
Softly, in the dusk, a woman is singing to me	166
Song's Eternity	162
Sound the Flute!	38
Spring	38
Spring and Fall to a young child	171
Star Light, Star Bright	101
Star light, star bright	101
Swing, Swing	92
Swing, swing	92

Symphony in Yellow	158	*Travel*	82
The Eagle	27	True Thomas lay o'er yond grassy bank	118
The Echoing Green	48	'Twas brillig, and the slithy toves	14
The Fairies	57	'Twas as the shores that round our coast	126
The False Knight and the Wee Boy	136	Tyger! Tyger! burning bright	26
The Ghost's Song	146		
The grey sea and the long black land	73	Under the wide and starry sky	181
The Great Silkie of Sule Skerrie	124	Up into the cherry-tree	80
The Herring Loves the Merry Moonlight	20	Up the airy mountain	57
The herring loves the merry moonlight	20	*Upon Westminster Bridge*	156
The Human Seasons	36	*Uphill*	81
The lights from the parlour and			
kitchen shone out	96	Wae's me! wae's me!	146
The Maldive Shark	21	*Waltzing Matilda*	144
The Night has a Thousand Eyes	115	*What Am I After All*	132
The night has a thousand eyes	115	What am I after all but a child, pleas'd with	
The North Wind Doth Blow	34	the sound of my own name?	
The north wind doth blow	34	repeating it over and over	132
The Owl	24	*What are Heavy?*	67
The Owl and the Pussy-Cat	12	What are heavy? sea-sand and sorrow	67
The Owl and the Pussy-Cat went to sea	12	What is song's eternity?	162
The Oxen	154	What wondrous life in this I lead!	160
The Power of Music	165	When cats come home and light is come	24
The Rainbow	32	*When in Disgrace with Fortune*	176
The Silver Swan	25	When in disgrace with fortune	
The silver swan, who living had no note	25	and men's eyes	176
The splendour falls on castle walls	52	*When That I was and a Little Tiny Boy*	140
The sun does arise	48	When that I was and a little tiny boy	140
The Swing	180	Whenever the moon and stars are set	35
The Tyger	26	When icicles hang by the wall	37
The Wind	33	*Where Lies the Land*	77
The Yarn of the *Nancy Bell*	126	Where lies the land to which the ship	
The Year's at the Spring	42	would go?	77
The year's at the spring	42	*Whether the Weather Be Fine*	30
There was a little girl, and she wore		Whether the weather be fine	30
a little curl	133	Who has seen the wind?	33
There Was a Naughty Boy	134	*Windy nights*	35
There was a naughty Boy	134	*Winter*	37
There was three Kings into the east	147	*Wynken, Blynken, and Nod*	99
Thomas the Rhymer	118	Wynken, Blynken, and Nod one night	99
To Emilia V–	168		
To see a World in a Grain of Sand	18		